This book belongs to :

The Trouble with Mice

Text © Pat Moon 1993
Illustrations © Peter Kavanagh 1993
First published in Great Britain in 1993 by
Macdonald Young Books

米奇鼠風波

Pat Moon 著

Peter Kavanagh 繪

賴美芳 譯

三民書局

Chapter One

It all began the day that Grandad came home with the cage. He found it on the pavement where it had been put out with the rubbish bags for the **dustmen**. Now it sits in the corner of the kitchen.

Mary sits at the table, where Mum and Nan are having a cup of tea. She **struggles** with **sticky**, sore fingers to push a needle through the stiff material of her **needlework** picture.

第一章

　　這一切全在爺爺帶回一個籠子的那天開始。爺爺是在人行道上發現這個籠子的。那籠子和垃圾袋一起放在那兒，要等清潔工收走。現在這個籠子被擺在廚房的角落。

　　瑪莉坐在餐桌前，媽媽和奶奶也在那兒喝茶。瑪莉努力地用她那汗濕了、弄疼了的手指頭和刺繡圖樣奮戰，她得把針穿過那硬繃繃的東西。

dustman [`dʌstmən] 名 清潔工
struggle [`strʌgl̩] 動 奮鬥
sticky [`stɪkɪ] 形 汗濕了的，黏的
needlework [`nidl̩ˌwɝk] 名 刺繡；女紅

It has to be finished for the class **display** on Open Day next week. It is meant to be a **butterfly** but her brother Chris says it looks more like a **pterodactyl**.

The more Mary works on her picture the more she thinks Chris is right.

這件作品得在下星期的教學參觀日前完成。原本想繡出一隻蝴蝶的圖案，但是哥哥克瑞斯卻說它像隻翼手龍。

　　瑪莉愈做愈覺得克瑞斯的話是對的。

display [dɪ`sple] 名 展覽
butterfly [`bʌtɚ͵flaɪ] 名 蝴蝶
pterodactyl [͵tɛrə`dæktɪl] 名 翼手龍

Mary looks at the cage. Its rusty **bars** are **dented** at the top, as if a giant has **trodden** on it. A square hole gapes where the door should be.

"Looks to me about as useful as a chocolate teapot," says Nan, **peering** over her teacup.

6

瑪莉看了看這籠子。籠子頂部生鏽的鐵條已經凹陷了，好像被巨人踩過一樣，而那四方形的開口應該就是門了。

　　「我看那東西是一點用處也沒有。」奶奶一邊說著，一邊從杯口往那兒瞧。

bar [bɑr] 名 柵欄；橫桿
dent [dɛnt] 動 使凹陷
tread [trɛd] 動 踩踏
　　（過去式 trod [trɑd]
　　　過去分詞 trod, trodden [`trɑdṇ]）
peer [pɪr] 動 盯著看

$\mathbb{M}$ary **pricks** her finger for the third time. She would like to cut the cloth into a hundred pieces.

She hears the back gate **crash** against its **latch**. Chris is home from school. He **ambles** in and throws down his bag, helps himself to a **mug** of tea and tips back on his chair.

Mary waits for him to **spot** the cage.

瑪莉第三次刺到自己的手指頭。她實在很想把那塊布碎屍萬段。

　　她聽到後門傳來閂門的聲音。克瑞斯放學回家了。他悠哉悠哉地走了進來，把袋子丟到地上，替自己倒了一大杯茶，然後整個身子往後斜坐在椅子上，還把椅子前腳騰空了。

　　瑪莉等著他發現那個籠子。

prick [prɪk] 動 刺，戳
crash [kræʃ] 名 巨響
latch [lætʃ] 名 門閂
amble [`æmbl̩] 動 緩慢地走
mug [mʌg] 名 馬克杯一杯的份量
spot [spɑt] 動 發現

"**W**hat's that?" he asks at last.

"Your grandad found it," says Mum.

"Cor, great," says Chris **examining** it.

"Now I can get my mouse."

"Oh no, you can't. I'm not having **vermin** in this house."

"But Mum..."

"And that's final."

"Go on, Mum. It's only a mouse. White mice aren't vermin. You ought to see Ben's. They don't smell, honest."

「那是什麼東西？」他終於問了。

「是你爺爺帶回來的。」媽媽說。

「酷！太棒了！」克瑞斯一邊研究，一邊說著。

「現在我可以養老鼠囉！」

「哦！不！不可以！我不准家裡養亂七八糟的動物。」

「但是，媽……」

「就這麼決定！」

「別這樣啦！媽。只是一隻老鼠嘛！白老鼠是無害的。妳該去看看小彬的老鼠。說真的，他們完全沒有騷味。」

examine [ɪgˋzæmɪn] 動 檢查
vermin [ˋvɝmɪn] 名 有害無益的小動物

All week he talks about mice.

He **straightens** the bars on the cage and
scrubs it out. And Grandad makes a little door
and **fixes** it on with **wire**.

整個星期他都在談老鼠的事。

他把籠子的鐵條弄直，並且把它用力地清洗了一番。

爺爺做了個小門，然後用鐵絲將它固定在籠子上。

straighten [`stretn̩] 動 使變直
scrub [skrʌb] 動 擦洗
fix [fɪks] 動 使固定
wire [waɪr] 名 鐵絲

"**P**lease, Mum. I'll keep it in the **shed**. You won't even see it. Mice are nice when you get to know them..."

"I'll give you mice if you don't shut up!" Mum **threatens**.

"Great!" he **yells**. "Then I'll go on, and on, and on, and on..." He **ducks** the tea-towel that she throws at him.

Mary knows he'll get his way: somehow he always does.

「求求妳，媽。我會把牠放在儲藏室裡。妳根本不會看到牠。如果妳能多瞭解老鼠一些，妳會發現牠們一點都不討厭……」

「如果你再不閉嘴，我就要揍你了〔賞你幾隻老鼠〕！」媽媽威脅他說。

「太好了！」他大叫，「那我就要一直說一直說、說、說、說……」他低頭閃過媽媽丟來的茶巾。

瑪莉知道他會想辦法弄來老鼠的，他總是有辦法。

shed [ʃɛd] 名 置物間
threaten [ˋθrɛtn̩] 動 威脅
yell [jɛl] 動 尖叫
duck [dʌk] 動（急忙地）低頭、彎身

Then on Friday at teatime,
Chris remembers
the letter from school.

It **informs** Mr
and Mrs Bryant
that Christopher
Patrick Bryant has won
a place at the Grammar
School.

Their father reads the
letter again, just to be **certain**.

"Well done, Chris," says Dad.

星期五喝下午茶時，克瑞斯想起學校寄來的那封信。

那是封通知布瑞恩先生、布瑞恩太太，克瑞斯多夫・派崔克・布瑞恩通過初中入學考試的信。

爸爸把信再讀了一遍，確定自己沒有看錯。

「很好，克瑞斯。」爸爸說。

inform [ɪnˋfɔrm] 動 通知
certain [ˋsɝtn̩] 形 確定的

"Ben's passed too," says Chris.

He **pauses** before adding, "They're giving him a new mountain bike."

He waits and watches.

His parents **swap glances**.

"A bike, eh," says Dad. "I don't think we could **manage** a new bike."

"There is something else," says Chris. "I wouldn't mind a mouse. Ben says I can have one of his **litter** for one pound fifty, and there'll be a few other things I'll need, like a feeding bottle and **bedding** and..."

「小彬也通過了，」克瑞斯說。

他停頓了一下，然後又說：「小彬的爸媽送他一輛新的登山腳踏車。」

他等著他們會說些什麼。

爸爸媽媽對看了一眼。

「腳踏車，嗯！」爸爸說，「我想我們沒辦法買新的腳踏車給你。」

「別的東西也可以。」克瑞斯說。「我不介意你們送我老鼠。小彬曾說過，我可以拿一鎊五十便士向他買老鼠；另外，我還需要一些其它的東西，例如餵食用的瓶子、老鼠窩，還有……」

pause [pɔz] 動 停頓
swap [swɑp] 動 交換
glance [glæns] 名 一瞥
manage [`mænɪdʒ] 動 設法弄到
litter [`lɪtɚ] 名 同一胎出生的小動物
bedding [`bɛdɪŋ] 名 （家畜的）乾草堆

"**W**ell, that's **settled** then," says Dad.

Mum **glares** at him and her mouth gathers like a **drawstring** bag. She starts to clear the table.

"**Filthy** things," she says. "Just you make sure it stays in that shed. I don't want its business in my house."

Grandad gives Chris a **wink**.

「好，那就這麼決定了。」爸爸說。

媽媽瞪著他，嘴巴閉得好緊，像個繫了繩子的袋子。她開始收拾餐桌。

「髒東西！」她說，「你一定得讓牠待在儲藏室裡。我不要讓這屋子跟牠扯上任何關係。」

爺爺向克瑞斯使了個眼色。

settle [`sɛtl̩] 動 決定
glare [glɛr] 動 怒目而視
drawstring [`drɔ‚strɪŋ] 名 束帶
filthy [`fɪlθɪ] 形 骯髒的
wink [wɪŋk] 名 使眼色

Chapter Two

Mickey Mouse moved in a week later. Chris has painted his name on to a **strip** of wood and he's fixing it to the front of the cage. A tiny pink nose is **twitching** at it through the bars.

"See," says Chris. "He knows his name already. Good boy. Mickey, Mickey."

第二章

一星期後，老鼠米奇來了。克瑞斯找了個小木條漆上他的名字，還將它固定在籠子的前方。牠那小小的粉紅鼻子從鐵條間伸出來，對著木板抽動著。

「看吧！」克瑞斯說，「他已經知道自己的名字了。乖乖。米奇，米奇。」

strip [strɪp] 名 狹長的一片
twitch [twɪtʃ] 動 抽動

He **offers** Mickey a seed.
"I'm training him, see.
If I repeat his name
every time I feed him,
he'll soon get the idea.
Mickey, Mickey."

He trains him to sit on his head, run up his **sleeve** and inside his shirt, sit in his pocket and walk along a length of **string**.

他給米奇一粒種籽。「我在訓練他，妳看。每次我餵他時就叫他的名字，不久他就會懂的。米奇，米奇。」

　　他訓練米奇坐在他的頭上，讓他跑到袖子上、襯衫裡，坐在他的口袋，還讓他走繩索。

offer [`ɔfɚ] 勔 提供
sleeve [sliv] 名 袖子
string [strɪŋ] 名 繩索

"**M**um'll kill you," says Mary when he takes him out from his pocket and sets him on the table. They watch him **wrinkling** his nose at a **bread crumb** and standing up on tiny feet, resting tiny pink **paws** against the jam jar.

Chris **scoops** him up and sits **innocently** with his hand beneath the table as Mum returns with the teapot.

「媽媽會殺了你。」瑪莉說。克瑞斯把牠從口袋裡拿出來放到桌上。

他們看著牠對著麵包屑皺鼻子，然後站了起來，粉紅色的小爪子靠在果醬瓶上。

媽媽拿著茶壺走了進來，克瑞斯趕緊把牠舀進手掌中，然後兩手放在餐桌下，若無其事地坐著。

wrinkle [`rɪŋkl̩] 動 使起皺紋
bread crumb 麵包屑
paw [pɔ] 名 動物的腳掌
scoop [skup] 動 掬，舀取
innocently [`ɪnəsn̩tlɪ] 副 無辜地

"**I** think I might get another mouse," he **announces**.

"Then you've got another think coming," says Mum.

"Ben's is having another litter. She had nine last time and he made nearly seven pounds. I think I might go into **business**."

"Not in this house, you won't," says Mum.

「我想我可以再養一隻老鼠。」他大聲說。

「你又在打什麼主意。」媽媽說。

「小彬的老鼠又要生一窩小老鼠了。上次牠生了九隻，小彬賺了將近七鎊。我想我也可以作這樣的生意。」

「不可能！你別作夢了！」媽媽說。

announce [ə`naʊns] 動 宣佈

business [`bɪznɪs] 名 生意，買賣

"**P**lease, Anna," begs Mary. "I'll show you Mickey Mouse if I can have one."

"All right, then."

Anna hands over a sherbet lemon and they **wander** out to the shed.

"I'm looking after him while Chris is at **scout** camp," says Mary.

She picks up a seed and calls, "Mickey, Mickey."

His whiskery snout **pokes** out from the dense bed of shavings he has made in the jam jar in the corner. He tests the air and **trots** over to take his **reward**.

「拜託啦！安娜。」瑪莉懇求著說，「如果妳分我吃一個，我就帶妳去看老鼠米奇。」

「好吧！」

安娜給了瑪莉一顆檸檬果凍後，倆人便往儲藏室走去。

「克瑞斯去參加童軍露營了，現在由我負責照顧他。」瑪莉說。

她拿起一粒種籽叫喚：「米奇，米奇。」

牠那長了鬍鬚的鼻子從厚厚的木屑堆裡伸了出來，這是牠自己用果醬瓶在角落鋪成的床。他嗅了嗅味道，便跑過來領獎品。

wander [`wandɚ] 勔 漫步
scout [skaut] 呂 童子軍
poke [pok] 勔 伸出
trot [trat] 勔 快跑
reward [rɪ`wɔrd] 呂 賞金，報酬

31

"**C**an I hold him?" asks Anna.

"I shouldn't let him out really."

"You're **scared**."

"Am not."

"You can have another sherbet lemon."

Mary turns the little **handle** on the cage door and scoops Mickey into her **palm**. He peers over the edge of her hand into the **abyss** below.

「我可以抱抱牠嗎？」安娜問。

「我真的不可以放牠出來。」

「妳害怕了。」

「我才沒有呢！」

「我再給妳一顆檸檬果凍。」

瑪莉將籠子的小把手轉開，把米奇舀到手掌裡。牠從她的手邊往下方望去。

scare [skɛr] 動 使害怕
handle [ˋhændl̩] 名 把手
palm [pɑm] 名 手掌
abyss [əˋbɪs] 名 深淵

"**Y**ou can stroke him if you like," says Mary.

"But I want to hold him."

"You might drop him."

"I won't."

"Promise? God's honor?"

Mary watches **anxiously** as Anna lets him walk up her sweatshirt and on to her shoulder.

"I've got to put him back now," **pleads** Mary.

"**Spoilsport**."

Mary returns Mickey to his **prison**, and sighs with **relief**.

「妳可以摸摸牠。」瑪莉說。

「但是我想抱牠。」

「牠會掉下去的。」

「不會的。」

「妳說的喔？不能騙人喔？」

安娜讓牠爬上了她的運動衫，還跑到肩膀上，瑪莉看得緊張個半死。

「我得把牠放回去了。」瑪莉求她。

「好吧！好吧！」

瑪莉把米奇放回牠的籠子，鬆了一口氣。

anxiously [`æŋkʃəslɪ] 副 擔心地

plead [plid] 動 懇求

spoilsport [`spɔɪˌsport] 名 掃興的人

prison [`prɪzn̩] 名 牢房

relief [rɪ`lif] 名 安心

Chapter Three

It can't be, thinks Mary. She stares in
disbelief. For a second she cannot move. She
closes her eyes and opens them again, hoping
she is wrong. But she's not. The door of
Mickey's cage is open. I shut it **properly**, I'm
sure I shut it properly, she thinks. But she can't
remember exactly.

She **slams** the shed door shut and **rushes** over
to the cage.

"Mickey! Mickey!"

Any minute now his twitching pink nose will
appear. Any minute now. "Mickey! Mickey!"

第三章

　　不可能，瑪莉心裡想。她不敢置信地睜大眼睛。有好一會兒，她動也不能動。她閉上眼睛，然後再張開，希望是自己看錯了。但是她沒有看錯。米奇的籠子是開著的。她心裡想：我有把它關得好好的，我確定門是關得好好的。但是她沒法兒清楚記得事情的經過。

　　她用力把儲藏室的門關上，衝到籠子旁。

　　「米奇！米奇！」

　　牠那不時抽動的粉紅色鼻子隨時會出現的，隨時會出現的。「米奇！米奇！」

disbelief [ˌdɪsbəˋlif] 名 不相信
properly [ˋprɑpɚlɪ] 副 恰當地
slam [slæm] 動 使勁關上
rush [rʌʃ] 動 衝

37

She peers into the cage, reaches her hand through the door, turning over the shavings. Then she lifts out the jam jar and **tips** it out, pulling with her fingers at the bedding. There are seeds and **shreds** of **lettuce** and **droppings**: but no Mickey.

The worst has happened. She has let Mickey escape. No, she thinks, the worst *hasn't* happened. The worst will happen on Friday when Chris gets back.

她往籠子裡瞄，接著伸手進去翻了翻木屑。然後把果醬瓶拿出來，倒了過來，用手指掏裡面墊著的東西。有一些種籽、萵苣的碎片和老鼠屎，可是就是沒有米奇。

　　慘了。她讓米奇給跑掉了。不，她心裡想，這還不算最慘的，等星期五克瑞斯回來後，那才真的完蛋了。

tip [tɪp] 動 倒出
shred [ʃrɛd] 名 碎片
lettuce [`lɛtɪs] 名 萵苣
droppings [`drɑpɪŋz] 名 （動物的）糞

39

She stands, shoulders **hunched**, hands **clasped** to her mouth. Please God, let me find him. Please!

"You were a long time," says Mum.

"I was cleaning up the cage a bit."

"Then you wash those hands this minute."

她站在那兒，聳著肩，手摀在嘴上。天啊！讓我找到牠，拜託！

　　「妳待在那兒有好一會兒了。」媽媽說。

　　「我把籠子清理了一下。」

　　「現在就去把手洗乾淨。」

hunch [hʌntʃ] 動 聳起
clasp [klæsp] 動 緊握

Mary keeps returning to the shed where she thinks she sees a little ear poking out over a flower pot, or a little tail from behind a watering can. But it is only a **scrap** of paper, or a piece of wire.

She starts to see mice everywhere. She worries about **treading** on Mickey, and she walks with her head down, staring at the ground.

瑪莉不斷來來回回往儲藏室跑。她以為自己看到米奇的小耳朵從花盆伸了出來，或是看到米奇的尾巴躲在灑水壺後。但那只是一小片廢紙或是一小段電線而已。

　　她開始覺得到處都有米奇的踪影。她擔心會踩到米奇，於是她便低著頭走路，眼睛盯著地上看。

scrap [skræp] 名 碎片
tread [trɛd] 動 踩踏

"What's the matter with you?" asks Mum. "You've a face like a week of wet Sundays. Have you been **quarreling** with Anna again?"

It is when she is coming back from the corner shop with the loaf of bread Mum sent her for, that she decides what to do. She runs towards the **pet shop**. She can't take too long or Mum will start to worry.

44

「妳到底是怎麼了？」媽媽問她。「看妳一臉慘兮兮的樣子。是不是又和安娜吵架了？」

她幫媽媽到轉角的店裡買了一條麵包。就在回家途中，她決定了該怎麼處理這件事。她跑到寵物店去，她不能逗留太久，否則媽媽會擔心。

quarrel [`kwɔrəl] 勔 爭吵
pet [pɛt] 名 寵物
pet shop 寵物店

She doesn't see the **tropical** fish and the
parrot that usually set her dreaming. She only
sees the cage of white mice. The **label** says
"WHITE MICE
£ 2.50 EACH".

Two pounds fifty?
Where is she going
to get two pounds
fifty before Friday?

WHITE
MICE
£2-50
each

她看也不看那些平常夢想得到的熱帶魚和鸚鵡，只注意著籠子裡的白老鼠。標籤上寫著：「白老鼠，一隻兩鎊五十便士。」

　　兩鎊五十便士？在星期五前，上那兒去籌兩鎊五十便士呢？

tropical [`trɑpɪkl̩] 形 熱帶的
parrot [`pærət] 名 鸚鵡
label [`lebl̩] 名 標籤

47

"**M**ary, this **change** is 20p short," says Mum as they sit down to dinner.

"I must have dropped it," **lies** Mary.
She keeps her head down to hide the **blush** of **guilt**.

Is keeping change as bad as **stealing**?
Even when it's for a good reason?
It feels the same.

"Oh, Mary, you must try to be more careful," says Mum.
It makes her feel even worse.

48

「瑪莉，找回來的零錢怎麼少了兩便士？」坐下來吃晚餐時，媽媽這樣問。

「一定是我不小心弄掉了。」瑪莉說謊。

她把頭低了下來，想掩飾罪惡感造成的臉紅。

收下找回的零錢是不是和偷竊一樣惡劣呢？即使是理由正當？可是感覺都是一樣的。

「哦！瑪莉，以後要小心點。」媽媽說。這反而讓她更有罪惡感。

change [tʃendʒ] 名 零錢
lie [laɪ] 動 說謊
blush [blʌʃ] 名 臉紅，羞愧
guilt [gɪlt] 名 罪
steal [stil] 動 偷

"**D**o you need any **errands**?" Mary asks Grandad.

"I'll want the afternoon paper, and I'm running short of **peppermints**," he answers.

"But it'll wait."

"I don't mind," says Mary. "I can go now — I might be busy later."

Mum looks at her **suspiciously**.

"Run upstairs then," he says, "and **fetch** a pound from my room."

「您需要我幫忙跑腿嗎？」瑪莉問爺爺。

「我要份晚報，還有我的薄荷糖也沒了。」爺爺回答。

「但是不急。」

「沒關係。」瑪莉說，「我可以現在去，待會兒我就沒有空了。」

媽媽用懷疑的眼光看著她。

「那就去樓上，」他說，「到我房裡拿一鎊去。」

errand [`ɛrənd] 名 跑腿
　　run errands 跑腿
peppermint [`pɛpɚˌmɪnt] 名 薄荷糖
suspiciously [sə`spɪʃəslɪ] 副 懷疑地
fetch [fɛtʃ] 動 把⋯拿來

There are pound coins, fifty pence pieces, tens, twenties and fives, all **arranged** in neat piles on the **mantelpiece**. They turn into rows of white mice with **curly** pink tails. She picks up a pound and runs downstairs. Grandad always gives her something when she runs errands.

"You **spoil** her," says her mother when Mary returns with the paper and sweets and he gives her a 20p.

那兒有一鎊、五十便士、十便士、二十便士和五便士的硬幣，很整齊地堆放在壁爐上。這會兒它們變成一排長了粉紅色捲尾巴的白老鼠。她拿了一鎊，往樓下跑去。每次幫忙跑腿，爺爺都會犒賞她。

　　瑪莉買回報紙和糖果，爺爺給了她二十便士。媽媽說：「你把她給寵壞了。」

arrange [əˋrendʒ] 動 整理
mantelpiece [ˋmæntl͵pis] 名 壁爐檯
curly [ˋkɝlɪ] 形 捲的
spoil [spɔɪl] 動 寵壞

In her bedroom, Mary lifts the **lid** off the **china** rabbit where she keeps her money and tips it out on to the bed.

She **counts** it carefully and then again, just to be sure. With Grandad's 20p and Mum's change of 20p it makes £1.50 altogether.

She still has to find a pound.

"Mary! I'm popping over to see your nan," calls Mum from the foot of the stairs. "Can you set the table for tea before I get back?"

在房間裡，瑪莉把陶瓷兔子撲滿的蓋子打開，將裡頭的硬幣往床上倒。

她仔細地數了一次，再算一次，確定沒錯。加上爺爺的二十便士，和媽媽的零錢二十便士，總共有一鎊五十便士。

她還得再去籌另外的一鎊。

「瑪莉，我要順道去看看妳奶奶。」媽媽在樓梯口喊著，「妳在我回來前幫忙把桌子和茶具擺好，好不好?」

lid [lɪd] 名 蓋
china [ˋtʃaɪnə] 形 陶瓷製的
count [kaʊnt] 動 計算

As soon as she hears the gate **click**, Mary rushes down. Grandad is in the garden bending over the lettuces. She pulls the **cushions** off the **settee** and **plunges** her hands down the sides and back. She finds a safety pin, a pencil, a **hair-slide**, half a biscuit and a whole 20p.

That leaves just eighty pence to find. Surely she can find the rest, just eighty pence?

56

一聽到門關上的聲音，瑪莉便衝下樓去。爺爺正在花圃裡彎著身子弄萵苣。她拉起長沙發椅的墊子，手伸到兩側和後面的縫裡。她找到了一只安全別針、一支鉛筆、一支小髮夾、半片餅乾和一枚二十便士的硬幣。

　　只要再找到八十便士就夠了。她一定可以找到的，只有八十便士而已，不是嗎？

click [klɪk] 图 咔嗒聲
cushion [ˋkuʃən] 图 椅墊
settee [sɛˋti] 图 小型沙發
plunge [plʌndʒ] 動 把…伸入…
hair-slide [ˋhɛr͵slaɪd] 图 髮夾

She tries all her pockets, her old purse, her **rucksack** and the pots on the kitchen **dresser** where she finds a 10p in the teapot that looks like a cottage.

Seventy pence now and she'll be all right. It's not such a lot. But at this moment it may as well be seventy pounds.

She sits on her bed, chin on hands, **trawling** her mind for places to look.

Then she remembers Chris's money box.

她翻遍了自己所有衣服的口袋、舊錢包、背包，以及廚房餐具櫃裡的鍋子。她在餐具櫃中一個小屋外型的茶壺裡找到了十便士。

　　現在，只要再七十便士她就沒事了。這不算多。但是現在卻好像七十鎊一樣。

　　她坐在床上，手托著下巴，心裡想著還有哪些地方可能可以找得到錢。

　　這時，她想起克瑞斯的存錢筒。

rucksack [`rʌk͵sæk] 图 帆布背包
dresser [`drɛsɚ] 图 餐具櫃
trawl [trɔl] 動 拖網

She reaches to the top of his cupboard for
the china pig with the cork **stopper** then tips it
on to the bed. She cannot believe it: a five
pound **note**, six pound coins, and **handfuls** of
50ps and other coins. She counts out seventy
pence and quickly scoops the rest back. She will
pay it back. As soon as she can, she will pay it
back.

她伸手到他櫃子的上方，把那個有軟木塞子的陶瓷小豬撲滿拿下來。她把撲滿往床上倒。她簡直不敢相信：一張五鎊的紙鈔，六枚一鎊的硬幣，以及一大把五十便士和其它的硬幣。她數了七十便士，然後趕緊把其餘的錢舀回去。她會還的，只要一有錢，她就會還的。

stopper[`stɑpɚ] 图 塞子
note [not] 图 紙幣 （美國用 bill [bɪl]）
handful [`hænd‚ful] 图 一把

61

Chapter Four

"Mickey! Mickey!" calls Mary as she holds a sunflower seed against the bars. But the new mouse has **buried** itself inside the jam jar.

Mary has not thought of this. She remembered to ask for a male mouse, and picked the one that she thought looked most like Mickey. But she had forgotten about Mickey's **acrobatics** and friendliness. This Mickey **squeaks** and **squeals** and **shakes** and tries to **nip** her finger.

第四章

　　「米奇！米奇！」瑪莉的手裡握著向日葵種籽，靠在鐵條旁，大聲地叫著。但這隻新老鼠，卻一直把自己埋在果醬瓶裡頭。

　　瑪莉沒想到會這樣。她記得她要的是隻公老鼠，而且她還挑了一隻她覺得和米奇長得最像的。但是她卻忘了米奇會表演特技而且不怕生。這個米奇不但不時發出刺耳的吱吱聲、顫抖著，而且還想咬瑪莉的手指頭。

bury [ˋbɛrɪ] 勔 埋
acrobatics [ˌækrəˋbætɪks] 名 特技表演
　　（單複數同形）
squeak [skwik] 勔 吱吱叫
squeal [skwil] 勔 尖叫
shake [ʃek] 勔 顫抖
nip [nɪp] 勔 咬

63

She carries him around in the garden, anxiously stroking him and repeating his name. She puts him on her sleeve, but he just **clings**, **quivering**.

She must have an answer ready. "He's out of practice," she will say. "I didn't take him out too much, just in case. You'll have to re-train him."

她把他帶到花園去，焦急地逗弄著他，還不斷地叫他的名字。她把他放在袖子上，但是他卻只是緊緊地抓著袖子，抖個不停。

　　她一定得想出個理由來。「他只是最近缺乏練習。」她會這樣告訴克瑞斯：「我怕他跑掉，所以沒有經常放他出來。你得重新訓練他。」

cling [klɪŋ] 動 緊抓不放
quiver [`kwɪvɚ] 動 顫抖

When Chris walks in from scout camp on Friday evening, he looks **as if** he hasn't washed for a week. Mum sends him straight upstairs to have a bath.

Mary waits **nervously** as she hears the water running into the bath. All too soon, he's out, clean and changed and running down the stairs. Then he's out through the back door and into the shed.

星期五晚上，克瑞斯從童軍營回來。他走進屋子裡，看起來好像一整個星期都沒洗澡。媽媽要他直接上樓去洗澡。

瑪莉聽著自來水流到澡盆的聲音，焦慮不安地等著。一切都太快了。克瑞斯一下子就洗好出來，他換好衣服，跑到樓下，穿過後門，跑到儲藏室去了。

as if... 好像…一樣
nervously [ˋnɝvəslɪ] 副 焦慮不安地

"**M**ickey, Mickey," she hears him call.

Surely they can hear her heart **pounding**? It feels as if any moment it will **burst** out of her shirt, popping the buttons in all directions.

Then, just seconds later, she can see Chris through the window, **leaning** against the sill, stroking Mickey. Then the mouse is running up his arm on to his head, and Chris has tied the string to the drain pipe and the mouse is **balancing** along as if he's been doing it all his life...

「米奇！米奇！」她聽到克瑞斯在叫米奇。

他們一定聽得到她怦怦的心跳聲吧！那種感覺好像她的心臟會隨時從她的襯衫裡頭蹦出來，把鈕扣震得到處都是。

過了幾秒鐘，她透過窗戶，看到克瑞斯靠在窗邊逗弄著米奇。不一會兒，小老鼠便沿著克瑞斯的手臂跑到他頭上。克瑞斯在排水管上繫了一條繩子，小老鼠就這樣沿著繩子平穩地走著，那副模樣就好像這件事他已經做了一輩子似的......

pound [paʊnd] 動 怦怦地跳
burst [bɚst] 動 突然衝出
lean [lin] 動 倚靠
balance [`bæləns] 動 保持平衡

69

It is true, thinks Mary.
Miracles do still happen.
And the pounding in
her **chest lessens** just
a little. She moves away
from the window.

But not very far, because there is a shout from
the shed and Chris is running out — and he has
two mice, one in each hand.

"I don't believe it," he's shouting. "Look,
Mum. There's two of them!"

這是真的，瑪莉心裡想著。奇蹟還是出現了。她怦怦的心跳聲稍稍減緩了一點。她離開了窗臺。

　　但是沒走多遠，就聽到儲藏室裡傳出一聲大叫。克瑞斯從那兒跑了出來，兩隻手上各放著一隻老鼠。

　　「我真不敢相信！」他叫著，「媽，妳看，有兩隻老鼠呢！」

miracle [`mɪrəkḷ] 名 奇蹟
chest [tʃɛst] 名 胸
lessen [`lɛsn̩] 動 緩和

Mum stops from hanging the **groundsheet** over the washing line to dry. She is studying Mary's staring face at the window. And Mary is trying to work out how and when Mickey The First might have found his way back to the cage.

"Mary! Come here this minute!" shouts her mother.

Slowly, Mary **edges out**.

"What do you know about this?" Mum asks.

Mary stares down at her **trainers**.

"Come on, Mary," says Mum. "I want an answer."

媽媽正在把露營用的防潮布掛到曬衣繩上晾乾。她停了下來,端詳著站在窗前眼睛大睜的瑪莉。瑪莉正想弄清楚米奇一號是如何、何時回到籠子裡去的。

「瑪莉,馬上過來。」媽媽大吼著。

瑪莉慢慢地走了出來。

「妳知道這是怎麼一回事吧?」媽媽問。

瑪莉低下頭盯著運動鞋看。

「快說,瑪莉,」媽媽說,「回答我的話啊!」

groundsheet [`graund,ʃit] 名 鋪地防潮布
edge [ɛdʒ] 動 緩緩移動
edge out (小心翼翼地) 慢慢出去
trainer [`trenɚ] 名 (橡膠底的) 運動鞋

"**I** thought he looked lonely, that's all," cries Mary her mind **spinning**. "I thought he'd like a friend. So I saved up and bought him."

Mum gives Mary a long look.

"Are you telling me the truth, Mary?"

Mary **chews** her lip.

"You should have asked me first, Mary," says Mum. "If you really wanted a mouse so much, you should have said so, not gone behind my back like this. I knew something was up."

「我覺得他看起來很寂寞，就是這樣，」瑪莉一邊大聲地說著，一邊在腦子裡編故事。「我以為他會想要個伴，所以我就存錢買了另一隻老鼠。」

　　媽媽看了她好一會兒。

　　「妳說的是實話嗎？瑪莉」

　　瑪莉咬咬嘴唇。

　　「妳應該先問問我的，瑪莉。」媽媽說，「如果妳那麼想要老鼠，直接說就好了，不要這樣偷偷摸摸嘛！我就知道一定有什麼事不對勁。」

spin [spɪn] 動 編造故事
chew [tʃu] 動 咬，嚼

Mary **narrows her eyes** at Chris who is silently watching from the path, holding the mice. She won't cry. She won't give in. Not yet.

"I'm very **disappointed** in you, Mary," says Mum as she **pegs** the groundsheet in place.

瑪莉瞇眼看著克瑞斯，克瑞斯正從小徑的另一頭靜靜地看著這一切，手裡還抓著老鼠。

　　她不會哭，也不會說出事情的真相。不會！

　　「我對妳非常失望，瑪莉。」媽媽一面對她說，一面把防潮布用夾子固定住。

narrow [`næro] 動 使變窄
　narrow one's eyes 瞇起眼睛
disappointed [,dɪsə`pɔɪntɪd] 形 失望的
peg [pɛg] 動 用衣夾固定…

77

But Mary is running, up the stairs and into her bedroom where she **sobs** till she has no tears left.

於是瑪莉跑到樓上的房間裡，嗚嗚地哭個不停，一直到流不出淚來。

sob [sab] 動 啜泣

That was five weeks ago. Two weeks ago, Mickey The First had a litter of eight, tiny, **naked** mice.

"She must have been a Minnie all the time," says Chris as he **alters** her name tag.

Mary decided she doesn't really like mice so she let Chris buy Mickey the Second from her for one pound fifty, but only after he'd agreed to **sharing** the money he got from selling the mouse babies.

那是五個星期前的事了。兩星期前，米奇一號生下了八隻光禿禿的小老鼠。

　　「她一定是米妮。」克瑞斯一面說，一面把她的名牌換了下來。

　　瑪莉弄清楚自己並不是那麼喜歡老鼠，於是就讓克瑞斯以一鎊五十便士的價錢將米奇二號買去。但條件是克瑞斯得與她平分賣掉老鼠寶寶的錢。

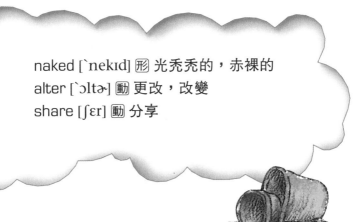

naked [`nekɪd] 形 光禿禿的，赤裸的
alter [`ɔltɚ] 動 更改，改變
share [ʃɛr] 動 分享

He's renamed Mickey the Second. There's a new name tag on the cage now. It says DENNIS THE **MENACE**.

The pet shop bought the mouse babies for 70p each, so even after Mary had **sneaked** back the 70p to Chris's money box and 20p to Mum's purse, she still had three pounds forty to put into her china rabbit.

克瑞斯替米奇二號重新取了個名字。現在籠子上掛的新名牌寫著：「小麻煩丹尼斯！」

寵物店以一隻七十便士的價錢買走了他們的老鼠寶寶。所以即使瑪莉偷偷把七十便士放回克瑞斯的撲滿，二十便士放回媽媽的錢包，她還有三鎊四十便士可放到自己的兔子撲滿呢！

menace [ˋmɛnɪs] 名 令人討厭的人
sneak [snik] 動 偷偷放入

Chris says he wants **hamsters** next but Mum says she is **definitely putting her foot down** about hamsters.

克瑞斯說，接下來他想要養倉鼠，但是，媽媽說她絕對反對到底。

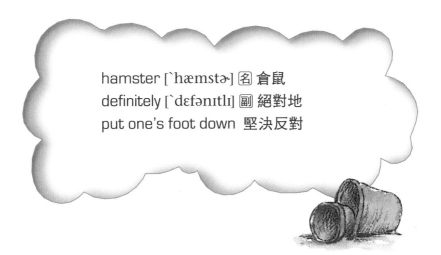

hamster [ˋhæmstɚ] 名 倉鼠
definitely [ˋdɛfənɪtlɪ] 副 絕對地
put one's foot down 堅決反對

每天一段奇遇、一個狂想、一則幽默的小故事
365天，讓你天天笑開懷！

伍史利的
大日記 I、II
——哈洛森林的妙生活

中英對照喔！！

Linda Hayward著／三民書局編輯部譯

　　有一天，一隻叫做伍史利的大熊來到一個叫做「哈洛小森林」的地方，並決定要為這森林寫一本書，這就是《伍史利的大日記》！日記裡的每一天都有一段歷險記或溫馨有趣的小故事，不管你從哪天開始讀，保證都會有意想不到的驚喜哦！

畫藝百科系列（入門篇）

一共26冊，每冊定價250元

全球公認最好的一套藝術叢書
讓你在實際觀摩、操作中
學會每一種作畫技巧
享受揮灑彩筆的樂趣與成就感

§油畫§人體畫§靜物畫§色鉛筆

§畫花世界§光與影的秘密

§選擇主題§風景油畫§噴畫

§動物畫§繪畫色彩學§建築之美

§繪畫入門§水彩畫§肖像畫

§風景畫§粉彩畫§海景畫

§人體解剖§創意水彩§如何畫素描

§名畫臨摹§透視§混色

§素描的基礎與技法§壓克力畫

國家圖書館出版品預行編目資料

米奇鼠風波 = The trouble with mice / Pat Moon 著；
Peter Kavanagh 繪；賴美芳譯――初版.
――臺北市：
三民，民88
　面；　公分
ISBN 957-14-3001-3（平裝）

1.英國語言―讀本

805.18　　　　　　　　　　　88004006

網際網路位址　http :// www. sanmin. com. tw

Ⓒ 米奇鼠風波

著作人	Pat Moon
繪圖者	Peter Kavanagh
譯　者	賴美芳
發行人	劉振強
著作財產權人	三民書局股份有限公司 臺北市復興北路三八六號
發行所	三民書局股份有限公司 地址 / 臺北市復興北路三八六號 電話 / 二五○○六六○○ 郵撥 / ○○○九九九八――五號
印刷所	三民書局股份有限公司
門市部	復北店 / 臺北市復興北路三八六號 重南店 / 臺北市重慶南路一段六十一號
初　版	中華民國八十八年九月
編　號	S85479
定　價	新臺幣壹佰陸拾元整

行政院新聞局登記證局版臺業字第○二○○號

ISBN　957-14-3001-3（平裝）